# THE LAD OF THE GAD

ALAN GARNER

# The Lad of the Gad

PHILOMEL BOOKS
*New York*

*for Natasha*

Copyright © 1980 by Alan Garner
First United States of America publication 1981 by
Philomel Books, a division of The Putnam Publishing Group,
200 Madison Avenue, New York, New York 10016.
Published in Great Britain 1980 by William Collins Sons & Co., Ltd.
Printed in the United States.

Library of Congress Cataloging in Publication Data

Garner, Alan.    The lad of the gad.
CONTENTS: Upright John.—Rascally tag.—Olioll olom.—
The lad of the gad.—Lurga lom.
1. Tales, Gaelic. [1. Folklore, Gaelic]    I. Title
PZ8.1.G167Lad    398.2'2'094115    80-13395
ISBN 0-399-20784-8

# Contents

2182279

# Introduction

*The Lad of the Gad* is a selective sequence of fairy tales taken from the Goidelic layers of British folktale. Rather than be all-embracing I have tried to show a strand of fairy tale that is of a special importance to me because it offers compensatory images of the world that I cannot find in a more conventional prose today.

The term "fairy tale" is used here to mean a traditional story of the fantastic and supernatural, and it is not, nor ever has been, a story for children only. Individual fairy tales may appeal to the very young, but the form itself is not juvenile, any more than folksong is juvenile because it can include nursery rhyme.

A fairy tale has no author. It derives from no source that we can identify, and from no known time. It may adopt the modality of a literature, the trappings of a history, the geography of a place, but the irrational forces from which its themes are composed come from the depths of imagination and are universal.

The telling of fairy tale, the relaying of tradition, must be a creative act. There is little more to be said. The rest is a balance of intuition and technique.

By depicting a personal obsession in a traditional frame, a storyteller reinstates the vigor of fairy tale, and, through the timeless, mediates the moment. The source then is within the storyteller himself, and the object of the telling is to be truly derivative, so that the energy may flow both ways.

By nature, fairy tale is oral rather than literary. It addresses itself to the ear rather than to the mind. Its first appeal is to a listener, and, since a listener is unable to stop and consider, as a reader may, the form of the tale is direct.

Oral narrative has marked characteristics. It is concrete and urgent. Plot evolves through physical action, and abstract concerns are kept in the listener's head by familiarity of repetition. Sustained argument is put aside. There is nothing to develop from incident to incident, no link to be made. And when discursive and analytical styles based on reason try to make sense of fairy tale, they render it mundane.

The clue is in the music. It is in the language: language at its most subtle, not phonetics, grammar, syntax or vocabulary, but the pitch and cadence of it all. The art is not to record the oral tradition but to recreate the effect of it, so that, for the reader, the printed word sings. I would suggest that, for the stories in this book to be experienced most fully, they should be read aloud.

Though it is interesting to pursue the significance of a fairy tale, the result is always less than the story itself. Here, to analyze is to limit. A fairy tale is its own interpretation, and it would be wrong of me to shackle any of the stories in this book by trying to explain them.

It would be wrong to explain the stories, but it may be right to say something about the difference between the nature of fairy tale and what, in the English language, it has become.

At the middle of the nineteenth century, the history of fairy tale in Britain could be summarized as follows: Traditional stories, that have existed in all times and in all places as the common property of all people, had been removed from their traditional tellers, the oral poets, and delivered up to child-minders and to scholars. In the nursery, fairy tales became tracts to support authority, with moral lessons inserted and the wilder elements tamed so that children should not be exposed to unseemly events. And in the academic world, the duty of the folklorist was to rescue and record, without concern for a popular audience, the stories that had survived.

But there were some scholars who wanted the fairy tale to live again, and two of them are of particular importance: Joseph Jacobs and Andrew Lang. Jacobs' influence lay in the quality of his writing, and Lang's in the scope of the material he made available.

Under Lang's editorship, a new corpus of fairy tale was given to English-speaking children, but his ability as a writer was less than his ability as a scholar. The achievement of Lang was that he extended, more than any other, the range of available fairy tales for his time.

Jacobs was a better scholar than Lang and a better

writer. Where Lang lacked urgency in his tales, Jacobs raced. Where Lang's prose was uniform, Jacobs changed his style to fit each story. Where Lang was international, Jacobs restricted himself mainly to British fairy tales. Together, the two men permanently enriched imagination. And both were rebuked by other scholars for this work. They were accused of having perverted fairy tale by adapting it for children.

There was substance to the charge. Lang and Jacobs were pioneers, but they were of the nineteenth century, and they allowed themselves to swerve towards moral instruction. To criticize Lang and Jacobs now, however, is to ignore the bias of an age. They were not the cause of the harm that followed them. Each generation accentuates naturally, through the concern of the storyteller, the qualities it finds important. Lang and Jacobs were not wrong to guard "the interests of propriety" and to take "what suited." The fault lay in those who came after. Fairy tales that may have been relevant to the nineteenth century have been repeated, often with less skill, in the same mold throughout the twentieth, relevancy unquestioned. What we call tradition is an amalgam of the court of Louis XIV, the Germany of Grimm and the sensibilities of late Victorian England. To get back to the eternally present world is the challenge now.

\* \* \*

The chief source for the stories in "The Lad of the Gad" is J. F. Campbell's *Popular Tales of the West*

*Highlands,* published in four volumes between 1860 and 1862, and I have chosen Campbell because he collected the stories from the last area of Britain to retain the unbroken oral tradition, so that what we have are texts that may be influenced by, but are not descended from, literature. Campbell's method of collection, too, was important. Popularizers, such as Lang and Jacobs, drew on scholarly texts, but they were seldom pure. Campbell, however, recruited native Gaelic speakers, who wrote down the words as they heard them from the storytellers.

When I first set about trying to bring Campbell's tales from the nineteenth century to the twentieth, I was interested to find that it was possible to keep much closer to the text now than it appears to have been for Jacobs. "Rascally Tag" and "Olioll Olom" in this book, and Jacobs' "The Story-Teller at Fault" and "Conal Yellowclaw" in his *Celtic Fairy Tales,* are treatments, respectively, of Campbell's "The Slim Swarthy Champion" and "Conal Crovi." In some places, I have been able to follow Campbell word for word; in others, I have deviated, brought in fresh incidents and altered the names of characters.

The final story, "Lurga Lom," is taken not from Campbell but from an Irish manuscript tale, "The Adventures of the Children of the King of Norway," translated by Douglas Hyde and published by the Irish Texts Society in 1899. Both the original manuscript and Hyde's translation are opaque, confused and dull. Here, far from keeping as close to the original as possible, I have all but abandoned it in order to recover the story from its own obscurities. It is a function of fairy tale to be reworked, and, in the working, we and it are changed.

A.G.
March, 1981

# upright
john

There was a king and a queen, and between them was a son called Upright John. The queen died, and the king married another.

One day John was at the hunting hill, and he got no game at all. He saw a blue falcon and let an arrow at her, but he did no more than to drive a feather from her wing. He lifted the feather, put it in his bag and went home.

When he came home, his stepmother said to him, "Where is the game today?" He took out the feather and gave it to her.

She said, "I set it as crosses and as spells, and as the decay of the year on you, and as the seven fairy fetters of going and straying, that you shall not be without a pool in your shoe, and that you shall be wet, cold and soiled, until you get for me the bird from which that feather came."

And John said to her, "I set it as crosses and as spells, and as the decay of the year on you, and as the seven fairy fetters of going and straying, that you shall stand with one foot on the castle, and the other on the hall, and that your face shall be to the tempest

15

whatever wind blows, until I return."

He went away to look for the falcon from which the feather came, and his stepmother the queen was standing with one foot on the castle and the other on the hall, her front to the face of the tempest, however long he might be away.

Upright John went, travelling the waste, but he could not see the falcon. He was by himself, and the night came blind and dark, and he crouched at the root of a briar.

A Foxy Lad appeared to him and said, "You are sad, Upright John. Bad is the night on which you have come. I myself have only a trotter and a sheep's cheek, but they must do."

They blew a fire heap, and they roasted flesh and ate the trotter and the sheep's cheek. And the next morning the Foxy Lad said to the king's son, "The Blue Falcon is with the Giant of the Five Heads, the Five Humps and the Five Throttles, and I shall show you where he lives.

"And my advice to you," said the Foxy Lad, "is for you to be his servant, nimble to do all that he asks of you, and each thing he entrusts to you, with exceeding care. Be very good to his birds, and he will let you feed the Blue Falcon. And when the giant is not at home, run away with her: but see that no part of her touches any one thing that is the giant's, or your matter will not go well with you."

"I shall do all these things," said Upright John.

He went to the giant's house. He struck at the

door.

"Who is there?" said the giant.

"One coming to see if you need a lad," said John.

"What can you do?" said the giant.

"I feed birds," said John, "and swine; milk a cow, a goat or a sheep."

"I want someone like you," said the giant.

The giant came out and he settled wages with John, and John was nimble and took exceeding care of everything the giant had.

"My lad is so good," said the giant, "that I begin to think he may be trusted to feed the Blue Falcon."

So the giant gave the Blue Falcon to Upright John for him to feed her, and he took exceeding care of the falcon. And when the giant saw how well he was caring for her, he thought he would trust him altogether, so he gave the falcon to John for him to keep her, and John took exceeding care of the falcon.

The giant thought that each thing was going right, and he went from the house one day.

Then Upright John said, "It is time to go," and he took the falcon. But when he opened the door and the falcon saw sunlight, she spread her wings to fly, and the point of one of the feathers on one of her wings touched one of the posts of the door, and the post let loose a screech.

The Giant of the Five Heads, the Five Humps and the Five Throttles came home running, and caught Upright John and took the falcon from him.

"I would not give you my Blue Falcon," said the giant, "unless you could get for me the White Sword of Light that the Seven Big Women of Jura keep."

And the giant sent Upright John away.

John went out again, travelling the waste, and the Foxy Lad met with him, and he said, "You are sad, Upright John. You did not, and you will not, as I told you. Bad is the night on which you have come. I have only a trotter and a sheep's cheek, but they must do."

They blew a fire heap, and they roasted flesh and ate the trotter and the sheep's cheek. And the next morning the Foxy Lad said to the king's son, "I shall grow into a ship and take you over the sea to Jura.

"And my advice to you," said the Foxy Lad, "is that you say to the Big Women that you will be their polishing-lad, and that you are good at brightening iron and steel, gold and silver, at burnishing and at making all things gleam. Be nimble. Do every job with exceeding care. Then, when they trust you with the White Sword of Light, run away with it: but see that the sheath touches no part that is of the inside of where the Big Women live, or your matter will not go well with you."

"I shall do all those things," said Upright John.

The Foxy Lad grew into a ship, and they sailed across and came to shore at the Rock of the Flea on the north side of Jura, and Upright John went to take service with the Seven Big Women there.

He struck at the door. The Seven Big Women came out and asked him what he wanted.

"I have come to find if you need a polishing-lad," said John.

"What can you polish?" said they.

"I brighten, make clear shining, gold and silver, or iron, or steel," said John.

They said, "We have a use for you," and they set wages on him.

He was nimble for six weeks, and put everything in exceeding order; and the Big Women said to each other, "This is the best lad we have ever had." Then they said, "We can trust him with the White Sword of Light."

They gave the White Sword of Light to Upright John, and he took exceeding care of it until one day that the Seven Big Women of Jura were not in the house, and he thought that then was the time for him to run.

He put the White Sword of Light into the sheath, and lifted it on his shoulder; but when he went out of the door, the point touched the lintel, and the lintel let loose a screech.

The Seven Big Women of Jura came home running, and caught Upright John and took the White Sword of Light from him.

"We would not give you our White Sword of Light," said the Big Women, "unless you could get for us the Yellow Horse of the King of Irrua."

John went out again to the shore, and the Foxy Lad met with him, and he said, "You are sad, Upright John. You did not, and you will not, as I told you. Bad is the night on which you have come. I have only a trotter and a sheep's cheek, but they must do."

They blew a fire heap, and they roasted flesh and ate the trotter and the sheep's cheek. And the next morning the Foxy Lad said to the king's son, "I shall grow into a ship and take you over the sea to Irrua.

"And my advice to you," said the Foxy Lad, "is that you go to the house of the king and ask to be a stabling-lad to him. Be nimble. Do every job with exceeding care, and keep the horses and the harness in exceeding order, till the king trusts the Yellow Horse to you. And when there is the chance, run away: but take care that no morsel of the horse touches anything that is on the inner side of the gate but the hooves of its feet, or your matter will not go well with you."

"I shall do all those things," said Upright John.

The Foxy Lad grew into a ship, and they sailed across to Irrua.

John went to the king's house. He struck at the door.

"Where are you going?" said the gatekeeper.

"To see if the king has need of a stabling-lad," said John.

The king came out and said, "What can you do?"

"I clean and feed horses," said John, "and I shine

tackle."

"I have a use for you," said the king, and he set wages on him, and John went to the stable, and he put each thing in exceeding order and took exceeding care of the horses, and fed them, kept their hides clean and sleek, and he was nimble with the tackle.

The king said, "This is the best stabling-lad I have ever known. I can trust the Yellow Horse to him."

The king gave the Yellow Horse to John for him to look after, and he looked after her until she was so sleek and slippery, and so swift, that she would leave the one wind and catch the other.

Then the king went hunting one day, and Upright John thought that was the time to steal the Yellow Horse. He set her with a bridle and saddle and all that belonged to her, and when he led her out of the stable and was taking her through the gate, she gave a switch of her tail, and a hair of it touched the post of the gate, and the gate let loose a screech.

The king came home running, and caught Upright John and took the Yellow Horse from him.

"I would not give you my Yellow Horse," said the king, "unless you could get for me the Daughter of the King of the Frang."

John went out again to the shore, and the Foxy Lad met with him, and he said, "You are sad, Upright John. You did not, and you will not, as I told you. Bad is the night on which you have come.

I have only a trotter and a sheep's cheek, but they must do."

They blew a fire heap, and they roasted flesh and ate the trotter and the sheep's cheek. And the next morning the Foxy Lad said to the king's son, "I shall grow into a ship and take you over the sea to the Frang."

The Foxy Lad grew into a ship, and they sailed across to the Frang.

The Foxy Lad ran himself high up the face of a rock, on dry dried land, and he said to John, "Go to the king's house and ask for help, and say that your steersman has been lost in a storm and the ship thrown on shore."

John went to the king's house. He struck at the door.

"What are you doing here?" said the king.

"A storm came upon me," said Upright John, "and my steersman was lost, and the ship has been thrown on shore and is there now, driven up the face of a rock by the waves, and I have not the strength to get her down."

The king and the queen, and the family together, went to see the ship. And when they looked at the ship, exceeding sweet music was heard in her.

> There were tunes with wings,
> Lullaby harps, gentle strings,
> Songs between fiddles
> That would set in sound lasting sleep
> Wounded men and travailing women

Withering away for ever
With the piping of the music
The Foxy Lad did play.

And the Daughter of the King of the Frang went on the ship to watch the music, and Upright John went with her. And when they were in one part, the music was in another, and when they were in that other, it would be elsewhere, and when they were there, they heard it on the deck, and when they were on the deck, the ship was out on the ocean and making sea-hiding with the land.

The king's daughter said, "Bad is the trick you have done me and bad the night on which you have come. Where will you take me now?"

"We are going," said Upright John, "to give you as a wife to the King of Irrua; to get from him his Yellow Horse; to give that to the Seven Big Women of Jura; to get from them their White Sword of Light; to give that to the Giant of the Five Heads, the Five Humps and the Five Throttles; to get from him his Blue Falcon; to take her home to my stepmother, the Bad Straddling Queen, that I may be free from my crosses and my spells and the sick diseases of the year."

"I had rather be as a wife to you," said the Daughter of the King of the Frang.

When they came to shore in Irrua, the Foxy Lad put himself in the shape of the Daughter of the Sun, and he said to Upright John, "Leave the woman here till we come back, and I shall go with you to the King of Irrua; and I shall give him enough of a wifing."

Upright John went with the Foxy Lad in the shape of the Daughter of the Sun, and when the king saw them he took out the Yellow Horse, put a golden saddle on her back, a silver bridle in her head, and gave her to John.

John rode the horse back to the Daughter of the King of the Frang, and they waited.

The King of Irrua and the Foxy Lad were married that same day, and when they went to their rest, the Foxy Lad gave a dark spring, and he did not leave a toothful of flesh between the back of the neck and the haunch of the King of Irrua that was not worried and wounded: and he ran to where Upright John and the Daughter of the King of the Frang were waiting.

"How did you get free?" said John.

"A man is kind to his life," said the Foxy Lad.

The Foxy Lad grew into a ship, and he took them all to Jura.

They landed at the Rock of the Flea on the north side of Jura, and the Foxy Lad said to Upright John, "Leave the king's daughter and the Yellow Horse here till we come back, and I shall go with you to the Big Women, and I shall give them enough of a horsing."

The Foxy Lad went into the shape of a yellow horse, Upright John put the golden saddle on his back, and the silver bridle in his head, and they went to the house of the Seven Big Women of Jura.

When they saw John, the Big Women came to meet him, and they gave him the White Sword of Light.

John took the saddle off the back of the Foxy Lad and the bridle out of his head, and he left him with the Big Women and went away. The Big Women put a saddle on the Foxy Lad, and bridled his head, and one of them went up on his back to ride him. Another went on the back of that one, and another on the back of that one, and there was always room for another one there, till one after one the Seven Big Women of Jura went up on the back of the Foxy Lad, thinking that they had got the Yellow Horse of Irrua.

One of them gave a blow of a rod to the Foxy Lad: and if she gave, he ran.

He charged with them through the mountain moors, singing iolla, bounding high to the tops, moving his front to the crag, and he put his two forefeet to the crag, and he threw his rump end on high, and the Seven Big Women went into the air and over the Paps of Jura.

The Foxy Lad ran away laughing to where Upright John and the king's daughter were waiting with the Yellow Horse and the White Sword of Light.

"How did you get free?" said John.

"A man is kind to his life," said the Foxy Lad.

The Foxy Lad grew into a ship, and he took them

all to the mainland.

When they had landed, the Foxy Lad said, "Leave the king's daughter here with the Yellow Horse and the White Sword of Light, and take me to the giant, and I shall give him enough of a blading."

The Foxy Lad put himself into the shape of a sword, and Upright John took him to the giant. And when the Giant of the Five Heads, the Five Humps and the Five Throttles saw them coming, he put the Blue Falcon in a basket and gave it to John.

John went back to the king's daughter, and the Foxy Lad came running.

"How did you get free?" said John.

"Ho! Huth!" said the Foxy Lad. "A man is kind to his life, but I was in the giant's hand when he began at fencing and slashing, and, 'I shall cut this oak tree,' said he, 'at one blow, which my father cut two hundred years before now with the same sword.' And he gripped me and swung me, and with the first blow he cut the tree all but a small bit of bark; and the second blow I bent on myself and swept the five heads the five humps and the five throttles off him. And there is not a tooth in the door of my mouth left unbroken for sake of that filth of a blue marvellous bird!"

"What shall be done to your teeth?" said John.

"There is no help for it," said the Foxy Lad. "So put the saddle of gold on the Yellow Horse, and the silver bridle in her head, and go you yourself riding

there, and take the Daughter of the King of the
Frang behind you, and the White Sword of Light
with its back against your nose. And if you do not
go in that way, when your stepmother sees you, she
has an eye so evil that you will fall a faggot of
firewood. But if the back of the sword is against
your nose, and its edge to the Bad Straddling
Queen, she will split her glance and fall herself as
sticks."

Upright John did as the Foxy Lad told him. And
when he came in sight of the castle, his stepmother,
with one foot on the castle and the other on the hall,
her front to the face of the tempest, looked at him
with an evil eye. But she split her glance on the edge
of the White Sword of Light, and she fell as sticks.

Upright John set fire to the sticks, burnt the Bad
Straddling Queen, and was free of fear.

He said to the Foxy Lad, "I have got the best wife
of the world; the horse that will leave the one wind
and catch the other; the falcon that will fetch me
game; the sword that will keep off each foe; and I
am free of fear.

"And you, you Lad of March, have been my
dearest friend since we were on the time of one
trotter and a sheep's cheek. Go now for ever
through my ground. No arrow will be let at you.
No trap will be set for you. Take any beast to take
with you. Go now through my ground for ever."

"Keep your herds and your flocks to yourself,"
said the Foxy Lad. "There is many a one who has

trotters and sheep as well as you. I shall get flesh without coming to put trouble here. Peace on you, and my blessing, blessing, blessing, Upright John."

He went away. The tale was spent.

# RASCALLY
# TAG

There was a king, and his name was Donald. And in the kingdom there was a poor fisherman, who had a son, and the son took school and learning.

The boy said to his father, "Father, it is time for me to be doing for myself to be a Champion." So he picked sixteen apples from the garden and threw an apple out into the sea, and he gave a step on it. He threw the next one, and he gave a step on it. He threw one after one, until he came to the last, and the last apple brought him on land again.

When he was on land again he shook his ears, and he thought that it was in no sorry place he would stay.

So he moved as a wave from a wave
And marbles from marbles,
As a wild winter wind,
Sightly and swiftly singing
Right proudly,
Through glens and high tops
And made no stops
Till he came to the city

And court of Donald,
And gave three hops
Over turrets and tops
Of court and of city
Of Donald.

And Donald took much anger and rage that such an unseemly ill stripling should come into the town, with two shoulders through his coat, two ears through his hat, his two squat kickering tattery shoes full of cold roadwayish water, three feet of his sword sideways on the side of his haunch, after the scabbard had ended.

"I will not believe," said the Champion, "but that you are taking anger and rage, King Donald."

"Well, then, I am," said Donald, "if I did but know at what I should be angry."

"Good king," said the Champion. "Coming in was no harder than going out would be."

"You are not going out," said Donald, "till you tell me where you came from, with two shoulders through your coat, two ears through your hat, two squat kickering tattery shoes full of cold roadwayish water, three feet of sword sideways on the side of your haunch, after the scabbard has ended."

And the Champion said:

"I come from hurry and skurry,
From the end of endless Spring,
From the loved, swanny glen:
A night in Chester and a night in Man,
A night on cold watching cairns.

## Rascally Tag

On the face of mountains
In the English land
Was I born.
A slim, swarthy Champion am I,
Though I happened upon this town."

"What," said Donald, "can you do, o Champion? Surely, with all the distance you have travelled, you can do something."

"I was once," said he, "that I could play a harp."

"Well, then," said Donald, "it is I myself that have got the best harpers in the five fifths of the world."

"Let's hear them playing," said the Champion.
The harpers played.

They played tunes with wings,
Trampling things, tightened strings,
Warriors, heroes, and ghosts on their feet,
Goblins and spectres, sickness and fever,
They set in sound lasting sleep
The whole great world
With the sweetness of the calming tunes
That those harpers could play.

The music did not please the Champion. He caught the harps, and he crushed them under his feet, and he set them on the fire, and made himself a warming, and a sound warming, at them.

Donald took lofty rage that a man had come into his court who should do the like of this to the harps.

"My good man, Donald," said the slim, swarthy Champion, "I will not believe but that you are taking anger."

"Well, then, I am," said Donald, "if I did but know at what I should be angry."

"It was no harder for me to break your harps than to make them again," said the Champion. And he seized the fill of his two palms of the ashes, and squeezed them, and made all the harpers their harps and a great harp for himself.

"Let us hear your music," said Donald. The Champion began to play.

> He could play tunes with wings,
> Trampling things, tightened strings,
> Warriors, heroes, and ghosts on their feet,
> Goblins and spectres, sickness and fever,
> That set in sound lasting sleep
> The whole great world
> With the sweetness of the calming tunes
> That Champion could play.

"You are melodious, o Champion," said the king. And he and his harpers took anger and rage that such an unseemly stripling, with two shoulders through his coat, two ears through his hat, two squat kickering tattery shoes full of cold roadway-ish water, three feet of his sword sideways on the side of his haunch, after the scabbard was ended, should come to the town and play music as well as they.

"I am going," said the Champion.

"If you should stir," said the king, "I should make a sharp sour shrinking for you with this plough in my hand."

The Champion leapt on the point of his pins, and he went over top and turret of court and city of Donald.

And Donald threw the plough that was in his hand, and he slew four and then twenty of his own people.

Well, what should the Champion meet but the tracking-lad of Donald, and he said to him, "Here's a little grey weed for you. And go in and rub it on the mouths of the four and then the twenty that were killed by the plough, and bring them back alive again, and earn for yourself from King Donald twenty calving cows. And look behind you when you part from me."

And when the tracking-lad did this, and looked, he saw the slim, swarthy Champion thirteen miles off on a hillside already.

> He moved as a wave from a wave
> And marbles from marbles,
> As a wild winter wind,
> Sightly and swiftly singing
> Right proudly,
> Through glens and high tops
> And made no stops
> Until he reached the town
> Of John, the South Earl.

He struck the latch. Said John, the South Earl, "Who's that in the door?"

"I am Dust, son of Dust," said the Champion.

"Let in Dust of Dust," said John, the South Earl. "No one must be in my door without entering."

They let him in.

"What can you do, Dust of Dust?" said the South Earl.

"There was a time when I could play a juggle," said the Champion.

"What is the trick you can do, Dust of Dust?" said the South Earl.

"Well," said the Champion, "There was a time when I could put three straws on the back of my fist and blow them off."

And he put three straws on the back of his fist, and blew them off.

"Well," said the Earl's big son, "if that is a juggle, then I can do no worse than you."

"Do so," said the Champion.

And the big son of the South Earl put three straws on his fist, and the Champion blew them off, and the fist with them.

"You are sore, and you will be sore," said the Earl. "My blessing on the hand that hurt you. And what is the next trick you can do, Dust of Dust?"

"I will do other juggles for you," said the Champion. And he took hold of his own ear, and lifted it from his cheek, bobbed it on the ground and back again.

"I could do that," said the middle son of the Earl.

"I shall do it for you," said the Champion. And he gave a pull at the son's ear, and the head came away with it.

"I see that the juggling of this night is with you," said John, the South Earl.

Then the Champion went and set a great ladder against the moon, and in one part of it he put a hound and a hare, and in another part of it he put a man and a woman. And they are alive there till now.

"That is a great trick," said the Earl.

"And I can not do that trick," said the Earl's little son.

"It is a great trick and a juggle," said the Champion, "and it is not you that can do it."

"Then what will you do now?" said the Earl.

"I am going away," said the Champion.

"You will not leave my set of sons," said the Earl.

But the Champion leapt on the point of his pins, and he went over turret and top of court and town, till he met a man threshing in a barn.

"I will make you a free man for your life," said the Champion. "There are two of your master's sons, one with his fist off, one with his head off. Go there and put them on again."

"With what shall I bring them?" said the man.

"Take a tuft of grass, hold it in water, shake it on them, and you will heal them," said the Champion. And he heard a loud voice in a bush.

"What is that?" said the man.

"I must go," said the Champion, "to the King of the Stars, whose foot no doctor or leech has healed in seven years."

> And he moved as a wave from a wave
> And marbles from marbles,
> As a wild winter wind,
> Sightly and swiftly singing
> Right proudly,
> Through glens and high tops
> And made no stops
> Until he reached the castle
> Of the King of the Stars.

He struck palm on door. "Who is that?" said the porter.

"I am a doctor and a leech," said the Champion.

"Many a doctor and a leech has come," said the porter. "There is not a spike on the town without a doctor's head, but one: perhaps it is for your head it shall be."

The Champion went in.

"Rise up, King of the Stars," he said. "You are free from your wound."

The King of the Stars rose up, and there was not a man swifter or stronger than he.

"Lie down, King of the Stars," said the slim, swarthy Champion. "You are full of wounds."

The King of the Stars lay down, and he was worse than he ever was.

"You did wrong," he said, "to heal me then spoil me again."

"I was showing that I could heal you," said the Champion. "Now fetch all the doctors of the earth."

And word was sent by running-lads to all the doctors and leeches of the earth. And they came riding, that they would get pay. And when they came riding, the slim, swarthy Champion went out, and he said to them, "What made you spoil the leg of the King of the Stars?"

"Well, then," they said, "if we were to earn the worth of our ointment and the worth of our trouble, we could not leave him with the worth of his leg in this world."

"I will lay you a wager," said the Champion, "the full of my cap in gold, to be set at the end of the dale. And there is none here that will be sooner at it than the King of the Stars."

He set the cap full of gold at the end of the dale, and the doctors laid the wager that it could never be, and put their lives on it.

The Champion went in where the King of the Stars was, and he said to him, "Arise, whole, King of the Stars. I have laid a wager on you."

The King of the Stars got up whole and healthy, and he went out, and in three springs he was at the cap of gold, leaving the doctors behind him.

Then the doctors and leeches asked that they might get their lives, and promise of that they did not get.

The Champion put his hat on his head, his holly in his fist, and he seized the grey adze that hung from his haunch, and he took under them, over

# The Lad of the Gad

them, through and amongst them, and left no man to tell a tale or earn bad tidings.

When the King was healed, he sent word for the nobles and for the great gentles to the wedding of his daughter and the slim, swarthy Champion.

"What company is here?" said the Champion.

"The company of your own wedding, and they are gathering from each half and from each side of the golden great white speckled universe," said the King to him.

"Be this from me!" said the Champion. And he went swifter out of the town than a year old hare.

> He leapt on the point of his pins
> And moved as a wave from a wave
> And marbles from marbles,
> As a wild winter wind,
> Sightly and swiftly singing
> Right proudly,
> Through glens and high tops
> And made no stops
> Until he reached the shack
> Of Rascally Tag.

"What young lad is this," said Rascally Tag, "his two shoulders through his coat, his two ears through his hat, his two squat kickering tattery shoes full of cold roadwayish water, three feet of his sword sideways on the side of his haunch, after the scabbard has ended?"

"Have you need of a man?" said the Champion.

"And where are you from?" said Rascally Tag.

40

"From many a place," said the Champion.

"What wages will you take?" said Rascally Tag.

"The wages I will take is that you shall not drink first before me until the end of a day and a year," said the Champion.

"That is your wages," said Rascally Tag. And he took the slim, swarthy Champion raiding.

The raiding was upon John, the South Earl, in the court and the city of Donald. And though the Champion had spared them before, he did not spare them twice.

He broke in the house wall, his holly in his fist, and he seized the grey adze that hung from his haunch, and he took under them, over them, through and amongst them, and left no man to tell a tale or earn bad tidings.

The Champion was hot, and went into the dairy, and saw Rascally Tag drinking a bucket of milk and water.

"You have broken your promise," said the Champion.

"That bucket is no better than another bucket," said Rascally Tag.

"That selfsame bucket did you promise to me," said the Champion.

And he took anger and wrath at Rascally Tag, and went away thirsty back to the King of the Stars. And the daughter of the King of the Stars picked sixteen green apples from the sea and made the slim, swarthy Champion a drink from the juice of them.

41

And the drink from that juice choked him.

So the daughter of the King of the Stars married Rascally Tag, and their wedding feast lasted a day and a year, and the last day was as good as the first.

And if there were better, there were. And if not, let them be.

# OLiOLL
# OLOM

There was a king, and he was king over England. He had three sons, and they went to the Frang to get themselves school and learning. And when they came back they said, "We shall see what there is since we went away."

The first place that they came to was a house of a man of the king, and the man's name was Conal Crovi.

Conal Crovi had every food that was better than another waiting for them; meat of each meat, draught of each drink. And when they had finished, the king's big son said, "Your wife must wait on me; your maid on my middle brother; and your daughter on my little brother."

This did not please Conal Crovi at all, but he said, "I'll go out and tell them."

And out he went. And he locked the door, and said to his servant, "Get ready the three best horses."

Then he put his daughter behind the servant on one horse, his maid behind his son on the second horse, and his wife behind himself on the third, and they rode to tell the King of England what an insult that set of sons had given to Conal Crovi.

The king's watching-lad saw them and said, "There are three double-riders on the road."

"It is Conal Crovi," said the king, "with my sons as prisoners. Well, if they are, I shall not be!"

So the king barred his door to Conal Crovi and would not hear him.

Conal Crovi said, "I shall make this kingdom worse than it is," and he went away and began robbing and spoiling everywhere.

"Catch me Conal Crovi," said the king.

"If I can get a day and a year," said the king's riding-lad, "I shall find out the place he is in."

"You have a day and a year," said the king.

The riding-lad took a day and a year, but he saw no sight of Conal Crovi. He set off back to the king, and, on his way, he rested on a pretty yellow hill, and there was a thin smoke rising out of the wood below him.

Conal Crovi had a watching-lad, and the watching-lad said, "There is a rider coming down alone from the yellow hill into the wood."

"The poor man," said Conal Crovi: "he is an outlaw as I am myself."

Then Conal Crovi had his two hands spread in welcome for the rider, and meat of each meat and draught of each drink, and water for his feet, and a bed.

The king's riding-lad ate, drank, washed and laid

46

himself down.

Conal Crovi said, "Are you sleeping, rider?"

"I am not," said he.

At the end of a while, Conal Crovi said, "Are you sleeping, rider?"

"I am not," said he.

A third time, "Are you sleeping, rider?" said Conal Crovi.

"I am not," said he.

"On your soles!" Conal Crovi said to his men. "This is no crouching time! The host is upon us!"

And there was a great company riding. But Conal Crovi had for arms one black rusty sword.

He began at them, and he did not leave a man there alive but the king's three sons. He tied them and took them in, straitly and painfully, and he threw them down in the peat corner, under the thatch drip.

"I shall do a work tonight," said Conal Crovi, "that was never done before."

"What work?" said his wife.

"The lifting of the heads from the king's three sons," said Conal Crovi.

He brought up the big one and set his head on the block.

"Don't, don't," said the king's big son, "and I shall take your part in right and unright for ever."

Conal Crovi raised the middle son.

"Don't, don't," said the middle son, "and I shall take your part in right and unright for ever."

He raised the little son, and the little son said, "Don't, don't, and I shall take your part in right and unright for ever."

Then Conal Crovi went, himself and the three sons, where the King of England was.

"It is Conal Crovi," said the king, "with my sons as prisoners. Well, if they are, I shall not be!"

And the king gave orders for Conal Crovi to be hanged at the next day.

There Conal Crovi was, about to be hanged, but the king's big son said, "I will go in his place."

"I will go in his place," said the middle son.

"I will go in his place," said the little son.

And the king took contempt for his set of sons.

"We'll put the world for our pillow," said Conal Crovi to the sons, "and make a ship to go to steal the three black white-faced stallions of Olioll Olom, and the kingdom will be as rich as ever it was, and your father's contempt will be lifted."

So they made the ship, and when she was ready they took the good and the ill of it on themselves and set their pith to her and put her out.

> Prow to the sea and
> Stern to the land
> Helm to the stern and
> Sail to the prow,
> Chequered flapping sail
> On the tall tough mast.
> Plunge of the eel,
> Scream of the gull,

## Olioll Olom

The big beast eating the beast that is least
And the beast that is least doing best as it may:
The bent brown buckie at the bottom of the sea
Plays haig on its mouth and glagid on the floor:
No yard not bent, no sail not torn,
Ploochanach, plachanach,
Blue clouds of Lochlanach,
All the way to Ireland.

Conal Crovi and the three sons drew the ship up
her own seven lengths on dry dried land, where no
wind could stain or sun could scorch, and they came
to the hall of Olioll Olom, King of Ireland.

They went to the stable, and Conal Crovi put his
hand on the black white-faced stallions, but they let
loose a screech, and, "Be out, lads!" said Olioll
Olom. "Someone is at the stallions!"

His lads went out, and they tried down and up,
but they saw no man.

"We have tried down and up," said the lads to
Olioll Olom, "but it is a fearful night with heaven;
fire and thunder."

They sat at the table, and again the stallions let
loose a screech, and, "Be out, lads!" said Olioll
Olom.

And still they found no one. "It is a fearful night
with heaven," said the lads.

Again the stallions let loose a screech, and, "Be
out, lads!" said Olioll Olom.

The lads went out, and they tried down and up,
but they saw no man. "There is no man," said the

lads, "unless he is hiding in the old barrel here beneath the cobweb of seven years." And they lifted the cobweb of seven years, and saw Conal Crovi hiding, with the King of England's three sons.

The lads bound them, and took them to Olioll Olom.

"Hud! Hud!" said Olioll Olom. "Conal Crovi, you did many a mischief before you thought to come and to steal my three black white-faced stallions."

"Indeed I did," said Conal Crovi. "And, by your hand, Olioll Olom, great king, and by my hands to free them, I have often been the worse than I am this night, your prisoner under your mercy, with a hope to live yet."

"Hud! Hud!" said Olioll Olom. "You may have come out of that: you will not go from this. But you shall have your two rathers."

"What are my rathers?" said Conal Crovi.

"Whether you would be hanged rather now or rather after a story."

"Rather after a story," said Conal Crovi, "if I may get the worth of its telling."

"Worth you shall get," said Olioll Olom, "except your life alone."

"Well, then," said Conal Crovi. "In a winter that was cold, on a day of hailing and snowing, sowing and winnowing, I was taking my way past a house that was there, and I saw a woman pulled apart with grief.

"'What is the matter?' I said to her.

"'The lady of this land is dead,' she said to me, 'and today is her burying, though her brother is from home.'

"The people were all at the burying, and I was amongst them when they put her in the grave. And they set a bag of gold down with her, under her head, and a bag of silver, under her feet.

"Well, I thought that gold and silver was of no use at all to her, so when night came I went back to the grave, and I dug it up.

"There I was, gold and silver in my fists, and I gave a pull at a rough stone to fetch myself out from the grave. But the stone fell on me, and a great stone it was, and I was there along with the corpse woman.

"And, by your hand, Olioll Olom, great king, and by my hands to free them, I was the worse then, along with the corpse woman, than I am this night, your prisoner under your mercy, with a hope to live yet."

"Hud! Hud!" said Olioll Olom. "You came out of that: you will not go from this."

Conal Crovi said, "Now give me the worth of my story."

"What is the worth?" said Olioll Olom.

"The big son of the King of England," said Conal Crovi, "and the big daughter of yourself, the two of them married and a black white-faced stallion for dowry."

"You shall have that," said Olioll Olom. "But how did you come out from the grave?"

"Am I to get the worth of my story?"

"Worth you shall get, except your life alone."

"Well, then," said Conal Crovi. "The brother of the dead woman came home, and he must see a sight of his sister. So the people had to dig her up again. And when I heard them digging, I said to them 'Oh, catch me by the hand!' And the man of them that would not wait for his bow would not wait for his sword, and I was as swift as any of them fleeing out from the grave.

"Well, there I was about the place, to and from, not knowing what side I should go, until I came on three lads and they were casting lots at the side of a hole in the ground.

"'Why are you casting lots?' I said to them.

"'What is it to you?' they said to me. 'Never mind. We'll tell you. A giant has taken our sister, and we are casting lots to see the which of us shall go down this hole to look for her.'

"'I'll cast lots with you,' I said, and I did, but the lot fell on me and the lads let me down the hole in a creel.

"Down I went, far and further than you could guess or I could tell, till there was the very prettiest woman I ever saw, and she was winding golden thread off a silver windle.

"'Oh,' she said, 'how did you come here?'

# Olioll Olom

"'I came down to look for you,' I said. 'Your three brothers are waiting.'

"'Then I'll go,' she said, and she stepped into the creel and was pulled up by her brothers.

"'Send down the creel tomorrow,' I called to her. 'And if I'm living, it's well: and if I'm not, there's no help for it.'

"Then I went through the cave and the dark towards a fire, and I heard thunder and noise coming with the giant. I didn't know where I should go to hide myself, but I saw a heap of treasure on the side of the cave, so I thought there was no place better than that, and I hid in it.

"The giant came with a dead woman trailing from each of his shoe-strings.

"He looked and he looked, and when he did not see the woman with the golden thread he let out a great howl of crying, and he gave the dead women a little singe through the fire and ate them.

"Then the giant said that he did not know what would best keep wearying from him, but he thought that he would go and count his lot of treasure. And from that he was only a short time before he set his hand on my own head.

"'Conal Crovi,' said the giant, 'you did many a mischief before you thought to come and to steal the pretty woman.'

"'Indeed I did,' said I.

"'And you shall polish my teeth with your sinews for it in the morning,' said the giant. And he slept after eating the women.

"I saw a great meat spit beside the fire, and I laid the iron point of it in the very middle of the ashes till it was red.

"The giant was in a heavy load of slumber, his mouth open so that I could count his lungs, his heart and his liver. And I took hold on the red hot iron spit and put it down in his throat.

"He made a spring and a leap across the cave, and he struck the end of the spit against the rock and it went right out through him, and that was him dead.

"And in the morning, the pretty woman and her brothers let down the creel to fetch me. But I thought I should fill it with the treasure of the giant; and when it was in the middle of the air under the hole, on the weight of all that treasure, the tie broke, and I fell down amongst stones and bushes and brambles and bones.

"And, by your hand, Olioll Olom, great king, and by my hands to free them, I was the worse then, in the giant's cave, than I am this night, your prisoner under your mercy, with a hope to live yet."

"Hud! Hud!" said Olioll Olom. "You came out of that: you will not go from this."

Conal Crovi said, "Now give me the worth of my story."

"What is the worth?" said Olioll Olom.

"The middle son of the King of England," said Conal Crovi, "and the middle daughter of yourself, the two of them married and a black white-faced stallion for dowry."

"You shall have that," said Olioll Olom. "But how did you come out from the cave?"

"Am I to get the worth of my story?"

"Worth you shall get, except your life alone."

"Well, then," said Conal Crovi. "There I was about the place, wandering up and down below, and I went past a house in it, and I saw a woman, and she had a child at her knee and a knife in her hand and she was crying.

"'Hold on your hand,' I said to her. 'What are you going to do?'

"'Oh,' she said, 'I am with three giants, and they must have my baby cooked for them tonight.'

"'There are three hanged men on the gallows,' I said. 'Take one of them down, and I'll go up in its place, and you'll cook that for the giants.'

"When the giants came home, one said, 'Turstar, tarstar, togarich!' The next said, 'Fiu, fau, hoagrich!' The third said, 'This is not child-flesh.'

"The first giant said, 'I'll cut a steak off the gallows, and we'll see which is the tender one.'

"And I myself was the body he chose.

"And, by your hand, Olioll Olom, great king, and by my hands to free them, I was the worse then, when the steak was coming out of me, than I am this night, your prisoner under your mercy, with a hope to live yet."

"Hud! Hud!" said Olioll Olom. "You came out

of that: you will not go from this."

Conal Crovi said, "Now give me the worth of my story."

"What is the worth?" said Olioll Olom.

"The little son of the King of England," said Conal Crovi, "and the little daughter of yourself, the two of them married and a black white-faced stallion for dowry."

"You shall have that," said Olioll Olom. "But how did you come from the gallows tree?"

"Am I to get the worth of my story?"

"Worth you shall get, except your life alone."

"Well, then," said Conal Crovi. "After they had eaten, the giants sl  . And I came down, and the woman gave me a great flaring flame of a Sword of Light that the giants had: and I was not long in throwing the heads off the giants.

"Then I myself and the woman were here, not knowing how we should get out of the cave.

"We went to the innermost end, and followed a thin road through a rock till we came to the day, and to the giants' harbour of ships. So I went back and loaded the treasure on a ship, with the woman and the child, and when all was aboard I took the good and the ill of it on myself and put the ship out.

"Prow to the sea and
Stern to the land,
Helm to the stern and
Sail to the prow,
Chequered flapping sail

On the tall tough mast.
Plunge of the eel,
Scream of the gull,
The big beast eating the beast that is least
And the beast that is least doing best as it may:
The bent brown buckie at the bottom of the sea
Plays haig on its mouth and glagid on the floor:
No yard not bent, no sail not torn,
Ploochanach, plachanach,
Blue clouds of Lochlanach,
All the way to a place I did not know.

"The ship and the woman and the child were taken from me, and I was left to come home as I might; though I am here today."

A woman, who was lying within, cried out, "Oh, Olioll Olom, great king, catch hold of that man! I am the woman that was then! You are the child!"

Olioll Olom sprang and cut every bond that was on Conal Crovi, and he took him into the company of his love and gave him the ship full of treasure.

The black white-faced stallions were sent to the King of England, and he lifted the scorn from his set of sons.

And Olioll Olom made a wedding night for his three daughters; leeg, leeg and beeg, beeg; solid sound and peg-drawing; gold crushing from the soles of their feet, the length of seven days and seven years.

# The Lad
# of the Gad

There was a king once, as there was, and will be, and as grows the fir tree, and he sat with his people on a green hill. And around him were his two sons, his warriors, his lads and his great gentles.

"Who now," said his big son, the Prince of Cairns, "in the four brown fourths of the wheel of the world would dare to disgrace you before your people, your sons, your warriors, your lads and your great gentles?"

"Are you not silly?" said the king. "He could come, the one who should put a disgrace on me. And if he did, you would not pluck the worst hair in his beard."

They saw then the shadow of a shower coming from the west and going to the east, and a warrior in a wet cloak and on a black horse was in it.

> As a hero on the mountain,
> As a star over sparklings,
> As a great sea over little pools,
> So would seem he beside other men
> In figure, in face, in form and in riding.

He reached over his fist and he struck the king

between the mouth and the nose, and he drove out three teeth, and caught them and put them in his pouch, and he went away.

"Did I not tell you," said the king, "that one might come who should put a disgrace on me, and that you would not pluck the worst hair of his beard?"

The king's big son, the Prince of Cairns, said, "I shall not eat and I shall not drink and I shall not hear music till I take off the head of the Warrior in the Wet Cloak."

"Well," said the small son, the Prince of Blades, "the very same is for me, until I take off the fist of the Warrior in the Wet Cloak."

The Lad of the Gad was there on the green hill that day, and he said, "The very same is for me, until I take out the heart of the Warrior in the Wet Cloak."

"You?" said the Prince of Cairns. "What should bring you with us? You? Why, you, when we go to glory, you will go to weakness and find death in a bog, or in rifts of rock, or in a land of holes or the shadow of a wall."

"That may be," said the Lad of the Gad, "but I will go."

The king's two sons went away.

The Prince of Cairns looked behind him and saw the Lad of the Gad following.

"What shall we do to him?" said the Prince of Cairns.

"Sweep his head off," said the Prince of Blades.

"We shall not do that," said the Prince of Cairns. "But there is a crag of stone up here, and we can bind him to it."

They bound the Lad of the Gad to the crag of stone and left him. But when the Prince of Cairns looked behind him he saw the Lad of the Gad following, with the crag on his back.

"What shall we do to him?" said the Prince of Cairns.

"Sweep his head off," said the Prince of Blades.

"We shall not do that," said the Prince of Cairns, and he turned and loosed the crag from the back of the Lad of the Gad.

"Two full heroes," said the Prince of Cairns, "need a lad to polish their shields or to blow a fire heap or something."

So they let him come with them, and they went to their ship and put her out.

> Prow to the sea and
> Stern to the shore,
> Hoisting the speckled flapping bare-topped sail
> In a wind that would bring the heather from
> the hill,
> Leaf from the wood,
> Willow from the root,
> Using it, taking it, as it might come
> Through plunging and surging, lashing
> The red sea the blue sea
> Fiulpande fiullande

About the sandy ocean
The ship that would split
A hard oat seed on the water
With her steering.

And for three days they drove her.

After the three days, "I," said the Prince of Cairns, "am tired of this. It is time for news from the mast."

"You are yourself the most greatly loved here," said the Lad of the Gad, "and the honour of going up shall be yours: and the laughter, if you don't, shall be ours."

The Prince of Cairns ran at a rush to the mast, and he fell down clatter on the deck in a faint with the lurch of the ship.

"That was no good," said the Prince of Blades.

"Let us see you," said the Prince of Cairns. "You show us better: and the laughter, if you don't, shall be ours."

Up went the Prince of Blades, and before he had half the mast he began squealing and squalling, and he could go neither up and neither down.

"Now you can't go up, and you can't go down," said the Lad of the Gad. "No hero warrior was I, nor half a warrior, and the esteem of a warrior was not mine. I was to find death in a bog, or in rifts of rock, or in a land of holes or the shadow of a wall. But it would be easy for me now to bring news from the mast."

"You great hero," said the Prince of Cairns.

"Try it."

"I am a great hero today," said the Lad of the Gad, "though I was not when leaving the town."

He measured a spring from the end of his spear to the points of his toes, and he ran up the mast to the crosstrees.

"What can you see?" said the Prince of Cairns.

"It is too big for a crow, and too little for land," said the Lad of the Gad.

"Keep watching," the princes said. And, after a while, "What is it now?"

"We have raised an island," said the Lad of the Gad, "and a hoop of fire around it, flaming. And I think that there is not one warrior in the great world that will go over such a fire."

"Unless two heroes go over it such as we," said the Prince of Cairns and the Prince of Blades.

"I think it was easier for you to bring news from the mast than to go in there," said the Lad of the Gad.

"It is no reproach," said the Prince of Cairns.

"It is not," said the Lad of the Gad. "It is truth."

They reached the windward side of the fire, and they went on shore, and they drew up the painted ship, the proud woman, her own seven lengths on grey grass, with her mouth under her. Then they blew a fire heap, and they gave three days and nights to resting their weariness.

At the end of three days and nights they began at sharpening their weapons.

"I," said the Prince of Cairns, "am tired of this. It is time for news from the island."

"You are yourself the most greatly loved here," said the Lad of the Gad. "Go the first, and try what is the best news you can bring to us."

The Prince of Cairns went and he reached the fire, and he tried to jump over it, and he went down into it to the knees, and he turned back, and there was not a slender hair or skin between the knees and the ankles that was not in a crumpled fold about the mouth of the shoes.

"He is bad, he is bad," said the Prince of Blades.

"Let us see if you are better yourself," said the Lad of the Gad. "Show that you shall have the greater honour: or we the laughter of it."

The Prince of Blades went and he reached the fire, and he tried to jump over it, and he went down into it to the thick end of the thigh, and he turned back, and there was not a slender hair or skin between the thick end of the thigh and the ankles that was not in a crumpled fold about the mouth of the shoes.

"Well," said the Lad of the Gad, "no warrior was I, nor half a warrior, and the esteem of a warrior was not mine. I was to find death in a bog, or in rifts of rock, or in a land of holes or the shadow of a wall. But if I had my choice of arms and armour of all that there is in the great world, it would be easy for me now to bring news from the island."

"If we had that arms and armour," said the

Prince of Cairns, "you should have them."

"Your own arms and armour are the second that I would rather be mine in the great world," said the Lad of the Gad, "though you yourself are not the second best warrior in it."

"But my own arms and armour are the easiest for you to get," said the Prince of Cairns, "and you shall have them. Now tell me what arms and armour are better than mine."

"The arms and armour of the Big Son of the Son of All are better," said the Lad of the Gad. "And he struck the fist on your father."

The Prince of Cairns put off his arms and armour, and the Lad of the Gad put them on.

> He went into his belts of thongs
> And his thongs of warrior,
> He went with leaping strides,
> Driving spray from puddle,
> Spark from pebble,
> His hero hard slasher in his hand,
> A sharp sure knife against his waist,
> Springing he sprung
> From the point of his spear
> To the points of his toes
> Over the fire of the island.

It was the very finest island he saw then, from the start of the world to the end of time, and he saw a yellow bare hill in the middle of it.

He raised himself up against the hill.

There was a treasure of a woman sitting on the

hill, and a big youth with his head on her knee, asleep.

"If I had a right to you," said the woman, "you should not leave the island."

"What is the waking for that youth?" said the Lad of the Gad to her.

"It is to cut the top joint off his little finger," said the woman.

The Lad of the Gad took the sharp sure knife that was against his waist and cut the little finger off the sleeping youth at the root. That made the youth neither shrink nor stir.

"Tell me what is waking for the youth," said the Lad of the Gad.

"Waking for him," said the woman, "is a thing that you cannot do; you, nor any one warrior in the great world but the Warrior of the Red Shield. And of him it was foretold that he should come to this island and strike the crag of stone here on this youth in the rock of his chest; and he is asleep until then."

The Lad of the Gad heard this, and a fist upon manhood, a fist upon strengthening, a fist upon power went into him. He raised the crag of stone in his two hands, and he struck it on the youth in the rock of his chest.

And the one who was asleep gave a slow stare of his two eyes, and looked at him.

"Have you come," said the one who was asleep, "have you come, Warrior of the Red Shield? Today and from now you shall own that name. But you will not stand long to me."

"Two thirds of the fear be upon yourself," said
the Warrior of the Red Shield, "and a little third on
me."

They went into each other's grasps, and they
fought till the mouth of dusk and lateness. The
Warrior of the Red Shield thought then that he was
far from his friends and close to his foe, and he gave
him a light lift and threw him against the earth: the
thumb of his foot gave a warning to the root of his
ear, and he swept the head off him.

"Though it is I who have done this, it was not I
who promised it," said the Lad of the Gad, the
Warrior of the Red Shield.

He took the hand from the shoulder, and he took
the heart from the chest, and he took the head from
the neck. He put his hand in the dead one's pouch,
and there were three teeth of an old horse in it. He
carried them with him. And he went to a tuft of a
wood, and he gathered a withy, and he tied on it the
hand and the heart and the head.

"Would you stay here, or come with me?" he
said to the woman.

"I would rather go with you yourself," said the
woman, "than with all the men of earth's mould
together."

The Warrior of the Red Shield lifted her onto
the shower top of his shoulder on the burden part of
his back, and he went to the fire and gave a dark
spring across.

69

*The Lad of the Gad*

The Prince of Cairns and the Prince of Blades were waiting, rage and fury in their eyes.

"What great warrior was that," they said, "chasing you, and you running away, till he saw such heroes as us?"

"There's for you," said the Warrior of the Red Shield, "a treasure of a woman, and the three teeth of your father, and the head, hand and heart of the one that struck the fist on him. Make a little stay for me, and I shall go back, and I shall not leave the tatter of a tale in the island."

He went away back, and at the end of a while he saw the speckled ship sailing from him, leaving him on the island.

"Death wrappings upon you," said the Warrior of the Red Shield, "a tempest of blood about your eyes, the ghost of your hanging haunt you. To leave me in an island of fire, and that I should not know what is to be done this night."

He went forward about the island, and saw neither house nor tower in any place. But at last there was an old castle in the lowest part of the ground of the island. And he saw three young men coming, heavily, wearily, tired to the castle.

They came in words of the olden time upon each other. And the three young men were his three true foster-brothers, and they went in pleasure of mind to the town.

They raised up music, laid down woe,
With soft drunken drinks

70

And harsh stammering drinks
And tranquil toasts,
Music between fiddles
That would set in sound lasting sleep
Wounded men and travailing women
Withering away for ever
With the sweetness of the calming tunes
That the warriors did play.

Then they went to lie down. And in the morning the Warrior of the Red Shield took his meat.

He heard the clashing of arms and men going into their array. It was his own true foster-brothers making the din.

"What are you doing?" the Warrior of the Red Shield said to them.

"We have been the length of a day and a year in this island," they said to him, "holding battle against Dark, son of Dim. And all we kill today will be alive tomorrow. Spells are on us that we may not leave this for ever until we kill them every one."

"I shall go with you today," said the Warrior of the Red Shield, "and you will be the better for me."

"Spells are on us," they said, "that no man may go with us unless he goes there alone."

"Stay inside today," he said, "and I shall go there alone."

He left his true foster-brothers, and he hit upon the people of Dark of Dim, and he did not leave a head on a trunk that they had.

71

He hit upon Dark of Dim himself, and Dark of Dim said, "Are you here, Warrior of the Red Shield?"

"I am," said he.

"Well, then," said Dark of Dim, "you will not stand long for me."

They went into each other's grasps, and they fought till the mouth of dusk and lateness. Then the Warrior of the Red Shield gave that cheery little lift to Dark of Dim and put him under and threw off his head.

Now there was Dark of Dim dead with his thirteen sons, and the battle of a hundred was on the hand of each of them.

The Warrior of the Red Shield was spoilt and torn so much that he could not leave the battlefield. He let himself down among the dead the length of the day.

There was a great strand under him below, and he heard the sea coming as a blazing brand of fire, as a destroying serpent, as a bellowing bull. He looked from him, and he saw coming from the waves a toothy woman, whose like was never seen.

The least tooth in her mouth would have been a staff for her hand and a stirring stick for embers. There was a turn of her nails about her elbows, a twist of her hair about her toes. She was not lovely to look on.

The hag came up the battlefield and there were two corpses between her and the Warrior of the

Red Shield. She put her finger in their mouths, and she brought them alive, and they rose up whole as best as they ever were.

She reached the Warrior of the Red Shield and she put her finger in his mouth, and he snapped it off her from the joint. She struck him a blow with the point of her foot and kicked him over seven ridges.

"You pert little nothing," she said. "You are the last I shall ever bring alive on this field."

And she came towards him.

But the Warrior of the Red Shield took the short spear of Dark of Dim and drove the head off the hag. And that was well, for only by her son's spear could she have been killed.

Then the Warrior of the Red Shield was stretched there, blood and sinews and bones in torment. He saw a musical harper walking on the battlefield.

"What are you looking for?" he asked the harper.

"I am sure that you are weary," said the harper. "Come up and set your head on this little hillock, and sleep."

He went up and he lay down. He drew a snore: and then he was on his feet, brisk, swift and active.

"You are dreaming," said the harper.

"I am," said he.

"What did you see?" said the harper.

"A musical harper, taking a rusty old sword to lift off my head."

Then he seized the harper, and he drove the brain

in fiery slivers through the back of his head.

And after that time he was under spells that he should not kill a musical harper for ever, except with his own harp.

He heard weeping about the field. "Who is that?" he called.

"Your three true foster-brothers," they said, "looking for you from place to place today."

"I am stretched here," he said, "blood and sinews and bones in torment."

"If we had the Great Dug of the World that the hag has, the mother of Dark of Dim," they said, "we should not be long in healing you."

"She is dead herself up there," he said, "and she has nothing you may not get."

And they said, "We are out of her spells for ever."

They brought down the Great Dug of the World and bathed him with the stuff that was in it, and he rose up, the Warrior of the Red Shield, as whole and as healthy as he had ever been. He went home with them, and they passed the night in pleasure.

The next day, the three foster-brothers looked out and they saw the Warrior in the Wet Cloak, the Big Son of the Son of All, coming to the town. And he was their true foster-brother also.

They went to meet him, and they said, "Man of my love, avoid us and the town this day."

"Why?" said the Big Son of the Son of All.

"The Warrior of the Red Shield is here, and he is

looking for you to kill you because of the fist that
you put over the day you took the three teeth from
the king's mouth."

"Go home," said the Big Son of the Son of All,
"and tell him to run away and to flee, or else I shall
take the head off him."

And although this was secret, the Warrior of the
Red Shield knew: and he went out on the other side
of the hall, and he struck a shield blow and a fight
kindling.

The Big Son of the Son of All went after him,
and they began at one another.

There was no trick done by shield man or skiff
man
Or with cheater's dice
That the heroes did not do:
The pen trick, trick of nicking, trick of notches,
The apple of the juggler throwing it catching it
Into each other and their laps,
Frightfully, furiously,
Bloodfully, groaning, hurtfully,
They would drive three red sparks from their
armour,
Driving from the shield wall, and flesh
Of their breasts and tender bodies,
As each one slaughtered the other.

"Are you not silly?" said the Big Son of the Son
of All, "To hold wrestle and combat against me?"

"How am I silly?" said the Warrior of the Red
Shield.

75

"Because there is no warrior in the great world alive that can kill me till I am hit above the top of my britches," said the Big Son of the Son of All. "And the king's three teeth are in my pouch. Try if it will be you that shall take them out."

When the Warrior of the Red Shield heard where the Big Son of the Son of All kept his death, he had two blows for the blow, two stabs for the stab, and the third into the earth, till he had dug a hole. Then he jumped backwards.

The Big Son of the Son of All, the Warrior in the Wet Cloak, sprang towards him, and did not see the hole, and he went down into it to the covering of his britches.

Then the Warrior of the Red Shield reached to him and threw off his head. He put his hand in the pouch, and he found the king's three teeth in it, and he took them with him and returned to the castle.

"Make a way for me for the leaving of this island," he said to his three true foster-brothers, "as soon as you can."

"We have no way by which you can leave," they said. "Stay with us for ever, and you shall not want for meat and drink."

"Unless you make a way for me to go," he said, "I shall take the heads and necks out of you."

"A coracle is here," they said, "and we shall send it with you."

"How shall I go in it?" he said.

"The side that you set the prow to, there it will

go," they said, "and the coracle will come back here of itself. And there are three pigeons for you, to keep you company: and they, too, will return."

He set the coracle out beyond the flames of the island, turned the prow to the known, the stern to the unknown, and made no stay till he came again to his own shore.

And if the coracle was quick in coming, it was quicker in going, and he set free the three pigeons as he left the strange country: and he was sorry that he had let them away, for the music that they had was beautiful.

There was now a great river between the Warrior of the Red Shield and the king's house.

When he reached the bank, he saw an old man.

"Oh, sir, stay where you are," said the old man, "until I take you over on my back, for fear the river should wet you."

"Are you the porter on the river?" said the Warrior of the Red Shield.

"I am," said the old man.

"Who set you here?"

"I shall tell you," said the old man. "A warrior struck a fist on the king and drove out three teeth, and his two sons went to take vengeance. There went with them a foolish lad, a little young boy, that was son to me. And when they went to manhood, he went to faintness. It was a sorry thing for them to make me porter on the river for the sake of that."

"Poor man," said the Warrior of the Red Shield, "that is no reproach. I myself was a lad before now. I shall not leave this town until you have justice."

The Warrior of the Red Shield seized and lifted the old man and set him sitting in the chair against the king's shoulder.

"Are you not silly?" said the Prince of Cairns. "To come to the town and to set that old wretch sitting at my father's shoulder?"

The Warrior of the Red Shield threw the Prince of Cairns against the earth and bound him straitly, painfully, and kicked him over the seven highest rafters that were in the hall, under the dripping of the torches and under the feet of dogs. And he did the same to the Prince of Blades.

A treasure of a woman, seated by the king, gave a laugh.

"Death wrappings upon you," said the king. "My two sons saved you from the island of fire, and you have been meat and drink companion to me for a year, and I never saw smile or laugh from you till now, when my sons are being disgraced."

"King," she said, "I have knowledge of my own."

"King," said the Warrior of the Red Shield, "what is the screech of a scream that I have heard ever since I came to the town?"

"My sons brought back three teeth," said the king, "and they have been driving them into my head with a hammer every day for a year, until my

78

head has gone through other with heartbreak and torture and pain. I think that they are the teeth of a horse."

"What would you give to a man that would put your own teeth into your head without hurt and without pain?" said the Warrior of the Red Shield.

"Half my land while I am alive," said the king, "and all my land together when I go."

The Warrior of the Red Shield sent for a can of water, and he put the teeth from out of his purse into the water.

"Drink this," he said to the king.

The king drank, and his own teeth went into his head, firmly and strongly, as well as they ever were, and every one in the place where it had first grown.

"I am at rest," said the king. "It was you that did the deeds of adventure, not my set of sons."

"He is the one," said the woman. "It was not your set of sons. They would be stretched to be seaweed seekers when he has gone to glory."

"Fetch faggots of grey oak," said the king. "I shall not eat and I shall not drink and I shall not hear music till I see my two sons burnt tomorrow."

On the morning of the morrow, the earliest on his knee at the king's bed was the Warrior of the Red Shield.

"Rise from that," said the king. "What could you ask of me that you would not get?"

"King," said the Warrior of the Red Shield, "it would be better to let your sons go."

"Why?" said the king.

And he said, "When I was the Lad of the Gad, no hero warrior was I, nor half a warrior, and the esteem of a warrior was not mine. I was to find death in a bog, or in rifts of rock, or in a land of holes or the shadow of a wall. But now I am the Warrior of the Red Shield, and I cannot be in any place where I may see the Prince of Cairns and the Prince of Blades both spoiled."

"What shall I do to them?" said the king.

"Do bird clipping and fool clipping to them, and let them go."

The king was pleased. Bird clipping and fool clipping were done to them, and they were sent out, the dogs and big vagabonds after them, each a shorn one and bare alone.

The treasure of a woman and the Warrior of the Red Shield were married, and agreed. And I left them dancing, and they left me, and I went away on a road of glass, over darkness and the foam of horses, till you found me sitting here within.

# LURGA
# LOM

Have you heard of the fame and the name that belong to Lusca, son of Dolvath, son of Libren, son of Loman, son of Cas, son of Tag of the kindred of Irrua?

One day the hero, the warrior son, went hunting on the Isle of Birds, to the north side of Irrua. He looked at the sea, and there was a boat coming to him with many striped sails on it. Lusca gripped his spear against the war hosts of the boat, but there came down a woman, alone, the most beautiful of women, and a red gold pin blazed at her shoulder.

The woman said, "I set it as crosses and as spells, and as the decay of the year on you, that you put neither stop to your foot nor pillow to your head till you search all that is high and all that is low in the seven red rungs of eternity to find the place where I am in."

Then the woman went to the boat, and the boat moved away over the back-ridge of the waves and the strong waves of ocean and the mane of the sea, so that Lusca did not know into what part of water or of sky that woman had gone from him. He himself went home from the Isle of Birds to the Town of the Heads in Irrua and sat in his chair. He gave a sigh, and the chair split around him and broke.

"It was the sigh of a man under crosses and spells broke that chair," said his father.

"It was," said Lusca.

"What is the cause of the sigh?" said his father.

"The cause of the sigh is that a thing in a boat came over the sea today. And," said Lusca, "I am in cow fetters to find her."

"I shall go with you," said the big brother of Lusca.

"I shall go, too," said the little brother.

"Let us meet our crosses and our spells," said Lusca, "and put neither stop to our foot nor pillow to our head till we search all that is high and all that is low in the seven red rungs of eternity to find the place where the woman is in."

Lusca and his brothers built a ship:

Every other plank
Blue plank
Red plank
Green plank
Black plank
Yellow plank
White plank:
Tent to the deck
Tent to the prow
Tent to the stern:

## Lurga Lom

Weapons in the place of throwing,
   Gold in the place of giving.

They took the good and the ill of it upon themselves, and put her out, and faced the flowing of the green sea.

And after they had reached the closeness of the waves and the heel of ocean they were looking around them, and they were not long in this when they saw the shadow of a shower coming from the west and going to the east, and a warrior on a horse was in it. The warrior twisted the tail of the horse about the mast of the ship, and set off, riding up and down about the world, with the ship behind. Sea and land were one to him.

"Go you," said Lusca to his big brother, "and cut the tail through with your sword."

The big brother went, and neither blade nor edge would cut the tail.

"Go you," said Lusca to his little brother, "and cut the tail through with your sword."

The little brother went, and neither blade nor edge would cut the tail.

"Try if you shall cut one hair," said Lusca to his brothers, "and I shall cut the rest."

But neither blade nor edge would cut a hair of the hair of the enchanted tail, and behind that horse they journeyed for a year.

On a day when they were travelling they saw a waterfall in the sky, and in it a venomous otter springing forward tremendously towards them through the waves. There was one kind of every kind of colour on her, her eyes flaming in her head, a blazing ball of fire in her throat. The warrior, when he saw the venomous otter, loosed the tail from the mast, the horse threw the water of the sea to the air, the venomous otter followed the horse, and they parted from the sons of the King of Irrua.

Lusca sailed the ship onward for another year until he saw the bulk of a land and the making of an island far from them. He faced the prow to the island and drew the ship up her own seven lengths on dry dried land, and went with his brothers about and through the green isle, but nothing did they find before they came to the middle of the isle, where there was a white castle, but they found no one, alive or dead, except a very wondrous cat, and that cat was herself playing about the pillars of the hall.

There was a table spread in the hall, and on it was every food that was better than another waiting for them; meat of each meat, draught of each drink; while in the air around there was a harp playing, but neither harp nor musical harper did Lusca and his brothers see.

The next morning, when they prepared to go from the castle to the ship, the cat stood at the threshold and would not let them pass, and the brothers were a second night in the castle, with meat and drink and music, yet no one did they see. In the morning they rose, and the cat stood at the threshold, and they were a third night in the castle. The next morning the cat stood at the threshold, and Lusca said, "The cat will not part with us. Let us go." So they went to their ship. "But I am sad," said Lusca, "to leave without the story of the very wondrous cat."

Lusca and his brothers gathered the fruits of the island and came to their ship and were a year sailing over the strong sea till they came to another island and went on shore.

There was music: there were crystal stones; lovely streams; noble tables at a kingly court. But no one did they find in it except a treasure of a woman, who, in shape and form and make, was like the one who had put crosses on Lusca. And when they met this woman she shed desperate showers of tears.

"What news?" said Lusca.

"What news from yourself?" said the woman.

"I give you news without disputing," said Lusca. He told her all the adventures until that time out.

"And my news is this," said the woman, and began to speak.

"A crowned king there was in the Land of Speckled Peaks. His name was Yohy Sharp-arm, son of Maidin. He had to him no children but two daughters only, and even they had not the same mother. The first daughter was Bright-eyed Faylinn; and if there were to be a single king over the three plunder divisions of the world, she would be his match of a wife, for there was not in her own time a woman of better beauty than she.

"The queen died, and Yohy Sharp-arm married another, the daughter of the King of Dreolann, and she bore him another daughter and no more. I am that daughter. Behinya is my name.

"Then my mother grew hatred against Faylinn, and took her to swim by the waterfall of Eas Bomaine. When Faylinn was in the water, my mother worked enchantment on her and put her under crosses and spells to be a year in the shape of a beast, and a year in the shape of another beast, and to go, beast into beast, and year into year for ever, unless a man should find her in her own shape, for she is her own shape on one day of every year, to give her grief at every other. And if a man should find her in the shape of a cat he should claim her. There is no doubt but that you found my sister upon that island. Free Isle is the name of that island itself, and Faylinn is the Cat of the Free Isle. But you did not know her."

"And that same Bright-eyed Faylinn is the woman who has me under fetters of going and straying to find her," said Lusca. "Is there no other way to fetch the woman?"

"There is no other. Crosses on the top of water are not forgiven. But go from here quickly," said Behinya. "This island belongs to one fearful-ugly-monstrous Fomor. Blacker than a coal of sally drowned in cold iced water is every joint and

feature of the Great Man. There is nothing of him
that is not black but his two eyes, and they are red.
He holds me here. I have never seen of the people of
the world, all the time I am on this island, but you
alone. The day he stole me from my father's court I
asked him to do me no harm till the end of a year;
and he has me for a year all but today, and, my
friends," she said, "go quickly from the Great Man.
You will not escape from him without death."

"I would not take the gold of the world and not
wait for tidings of the Fomor," said Lusca.

At once they saw him coming; the Fomor; the
Great Man, This was the way of him.

> There were the skins of horned deer clashing
>     on him
> And a thick iron club in his round hand.
> Seven sides upon the club,
> Edge of a razor on every side of seven,
> And seven chains about,
> An iron apple-knob on every chain of seven,
> And seven spikes about.
> He never left horror or wild creature
> Or senseless spectre in crag
> Or hollow or rock or river mouth
> That he did not rouse
> With the noise that club did play.

And when the Fomor saw the sons of Irrua he
gave a yell and a laugh of laughter, so that they
could count the inside of him with all the opening
he gave to his mouth.

Behinya changed shapeliness for misshape, loveliness for unloveliness, with fear for those bright-formed lads falling by the Great Man.

Then Lusca said, "May life be neither good nor pleasant to you, and may the house neither of sun or of moon give welcome before or behind you, hideous Fomor."

And he rose,
The mantle beyond border,
The flood without ebb
And the torrent without breaking,
The champion who never gave back
One single foot
Before few or before many
In battle or in conflict
Went into his belts of thongs
And his thongs of warrior,
Making marsh of the rock
And rock of the marsh,
Until he gave the Fomor
The merry little heave
And threw him on his back.

"The fruit of vigour and valour to you, son of the King of Irrua," said the Great Man, "in the mouths of poets and readers of flags for ever, and do not put me to death."

"I swear before my thongs," said Lusca, "if the gold of the world were given to me I would not accept it, if I were not to take the head from you." He struck the Fomor at the joining of the neck, and the head fell from the body.

Lusca and his brothers made ready the ship and straight without staying they left Behinya on the island, and voyaged over the stream of the sea, and journied through the thick red waves, for five years of their time, seeking the Cat of the Free Isle. But they did not find her.

Now, on a certain day that they were listening to the noises of the sea, they saw a ship with speckled sails coming towards them, and a single royal young warrior in the prow of that ship. He had a sickle of thick iron in his hand, and he reached out the sickle and lifted the ship of the sons of the King of Irrua high above the sea.

Lusca said to his brothers, "This is no crouching time."

They drew their three swords, and hit three blows each man of them on the sail mast of the ship, so that they cut the mast upon the spot and the ship fell again to the bitter waters.

"My joy it is," said the young warrior, "sons of the King of Irrua, to have combat with you."

"Your joy it shall be," said Lusca, "if we did but know with whom is the combat."

"I am the Big Mokkalve, son of the King of Sorcha," said the young warrior. "Grey-visioned will be good heroes, sad-palmed the maidens, wet-eyed the queens when this day is done."

But, away to the Lands of Sorcha, there was a wizard. The Manach was his name. And it was revealed at that instant to the Manach that death and the young warrior were to meet on the sword of Lusca; that Manach was himself the man of most desperate enchantment of all who came in his own time.

The Manach took his harrow-wheel of holly, and he got upon it, and he rose to the sky and put a dark fog of magic round about the ship of the Big Mokkalve, until he stole away the Big Mokkalve with him through that desperate fog.

When the water-mist cleared, the sons of the King of Irrua looked at the ship and were sad that a man should go from them without dying.

"What are we going to do now?" said Lusca.

"We are to find the cat," said his big brother.

"We are to free you from your crosses and your spells, the decay and sad misfortunes of the year," said his little brother.

"That is not my advice to you," said Lusca. "We shall go to the Lands of Sorcha and give battle to the Big Mokkalve; for he came on us to avenge the killing of his father by our father, and he will not be stopped with enchantments."

Then the sea stood up in wrestle and dispute with the ship, in green waves, rough and laughing; but when it found no weakness in the warriors nor terror in the young men, there dwelt a blossom of peace over the sea, and Lusca and his brothers came blithely to the Lands of Sorcha. They pulled the ship up her own seven lengths on grey grass, and left her, and took their weapons against the hosts of Sorcha.

They were not long there when they saw one youth coming towards them. He had the garland of a poet around his head, a fair purple-bordered cloak about him, and a wand of white silver in his hand.

"It is not well, Lusca. And my advice to you," said the youth, "is that it would be better now to turn again. I think it a sad pity, the thing you seek to do."

"What is it that I seek to do?" said Lusca.

"To give furious, high-headed battle is what you seek to do," said the youth.

"What is your name, poet?" said Lusca.

"My name," said the youth, "is the Kurrirya Crookfoot, and I think it a sad pity that the two I love best are to fall together this day."

"What is your friendship with us?" said Lusca.

"Your share of me," said the Kurrirya Crookfoot, "is that my mother was a daughter of Irrua. And in very truth I have given to you the love of my soul."

"No less for that," said Lusca, "go you and proclaim battle against the Big Mokkalve and the hosts of Sorcha."

The Kurrirya said, "It is a rope around sand, or the closing of the palm at a sunbeam, or it is heat against boiling, for you to meet the Big Mokkalve and the hosts of Sorcha."

"Lay aside your silly talk," said Lusca. He put his

hand into the hollow of his shield and he took out a ridged and polished lump of gold, and gave the gold to the poet. The Kurrirya took it and threw the gold on the ground.

"Are you refusing the gold?" said Lusca.

"I am not refusing," said the Kurrirya, "but it is sad grief to me that the two I love best must fall here today."

The Kurrirya Crookfoot left Lusca and his brothers and went to the hosts of Sorcha and to the Big Mokkalve. He said:

> "Though plentiful your battalions;
> Though warlike your champions;
> Though valorous your warriors;
> Yet valorless shall be your champions;
> And weak your battalions;
> And cowardly your warriors;
> And unguideful your strong ones;
> And thin your heavy hosts;
> And dispersed your war-bands;
> And unvalorous your well-born bands;
> And championless your young kings.
> In the hands of Irrua."

But the Big Mokkalve took no notice. The Kurrirya went back to the hill where he had left the sons of the King of Irrua.

"What news?" said Lusca.

"Never were created woods, however close," said the Kurrirya, "that the covering of the purple iron above the heads of the hosts is not closer still."

Then Lusca gripped his spear against the hosts of
Sorcha, and struck a shield blow and a fight
kindling, so that there was neither a stone nor a tree
but was in one quivering from him, and cowards
went into trances of death from that great sound.
He gave a kingly rush through the ranks of Sorcha,
and neither loving nor friendly was the welcome.
On the breaking of blue javelins even dear friends
would not trust one man more than another, for the
quickness of their striking and for the blood in their
faces; but those who know say that fifty armed men
went to madness with the wind at the sound of
Lusca as he brought signs of death and shortness of
life towards the Big Mokkalve, son of the King of
Sorcha.

Yet all the more for that did Lusca remember the
Manach, how he had brought enchantment of fog
on his harrow-wheel of holly, and he looked with
exceeding care. He saw the Manach, as a hideous
giant, coming through the battle, fierce, red,
stripped. Lusca reached into the hollow of his shield
and took from it an apple-ball of iron and gave it a
choice cast at the giant into the middle of the head
and the face. The iron apple took its own size of
brain out in fiery slivers through the back of the
head of the Manach, and the giant let loose the
screech of a scream and turned back the way he had
come.

It was then Lusca found the Big Mokkalve and
dealt him a blow that split the golden helmet on the

head. The Big Mokkalve gave another blow to
Lusca, and split his shield and put him down on his
left knee, and with his sword opened a gate in the
side of Lusca. But Lusca sprang and put a second
blow, and of that blow he took the head and the
right hand off the Big Mokkalve.

Lusca lifted his helmet, seeking air; and there was
at that hour a dark mist above the battle. He looked
through the battle and wondered that he did not
hear the noise of his brothers in it, and he went to
seek them over a closeness of bodies so tight that it
would not let blood pools walk and he was under
rough-voiced creatures of the sky.

He found his big brother killed in the middle of
the battle, his little brother killed near him, and the
Kurrirya killed beyond that. He dug them a deep,
long, wide grave, made a bed there of green water
cresses, and laid them together on it and carved their
names in flags above, to put them in remembrance,
and in knowledge and poetry, for fear lest a
drowning or lasting death of memory should go
round upon them for ever. Then he went about the
battle again, but it was vain for him, for there was
never a body to tell tidings but was slain a long time
before that.

Lusca gathered a heap of dead men for shelter
against the dark night, and he sat down in his
bleeding upon a rock. "Until today," said Lusca, "I
have never been alone."

A swan flew in from the open sea and swam on

the blood. "I think it a sad pity the way I see you, son of the King of Irrua," said the swan.

"Is it human speech in your mouth?" said Lusca. "If you have chanced on human speech, give me news."

"If I were as you are now," said the swan, "I should get that balm of healing, the Great Dug of the World, for my kindred."

Lusca said, "Where shall I get the balm of healing? Is there a bolt for the gate of my side? How shall I close the blue mouth?"

The swan rose up and flew back over the sea, and, as it went, it said to Lusca:

"I have no skill in the matter of your anguish.
I cannot grasp the flame of agony.
I cannot stop the dark blood.
I am the Swan of Sorcha.
I am the Otter of the Waterfall.
I am the Cat of the Free Isle.

I am not the worst of women."

Lusca took branches, rods of the thicket, of long wood, and he lit a tower of fire. And the darkness fell on Lusca; and the desolation.

But a short time after that work he saw a hag coming towards him. The hair of her body was touching the earth. One of her eyes was her breastpin. One of her teeth was her staff. She had one jointed sharp foot under her; and she sat upon the other side of the fire.

The hag said, "You are alone, son of Irrua. Bad is the night on which you have come."

"I am not alone, hag," said Lusca. "I have you."

"It is not you who have me," said the hag, "but I who have you, unless you pay me tribute."

"What tribute is that?" said Lusca.

"The length of my foot of fair gold," said the hag.

"Will you not take silver of me?" said Lusca.

"I will not," said the hag.

"For what cause," said Lusca, "do you have that tribute abroad on everyone?"

"This hill is my hill," said the hag, "and the man that makes fire on my hill is my man; and I must have ransom of gold or ransom of the head of the man himself or would you spend this night with me?"

"If a hag more ugly than you," said Lusca, "were to offer me rest I should accept it this night."

Lusca shook from him his suit of battle. The hag gave a goblet of precious stones into his hand, and he drank a drink out of that goblet.

"Take a blessing and a victory for the drink," said Lusca.

The hag said, "Whatever man shall drink from that goblet every day, neither age nor misery rest upon him through time eternal."

Lusca said, "Is it the balm of healing?"

The hag said:

"It is not the balm of healing,

98

Nor the Great Dug of the World.
It will not bolt the gate of your side.
It will not close the blue mouth.
It will not stop the dark blood.
Only the maker of iron
Can seal the road that iron makes.
I have no skill in the matter of your anguish.
I cannot grasp the flame of agony.
Look for a man
Born on a black rock
Grown on a burnt hill:
Shasval the Smith:
Born at night, in the Upland of Grief
He walks on boundaries, on the wolf's track,
He hammers the moon."

Lusca said, "How shall I find the Upland of Grief?"

"There is a cave below here," said the hag. "The Upland of Grief is by that way."

Lusca rested the night with the hag, and no one was earlier on his feet the next day than he. He went down to the cave and found it open, a thin road in it. He followed the road until he came to a smooth plain and a little yellow island and a sea on each side of it. He went up the island, and in the middle of it he chanced upon a fair lake. A beautiful flock of bright-white birds was ever-rising out of the middle of the lake, and never a bird of them was going down again, but always they were rising up.

Lusca said, "What is the place that bright birds

come from?"

He lay on the lake and went under it to the bed and the gravel. He looked about to a tower of gold at a distance from him, and he went up and entered.

There was a girl in a room of the tower, a covering upon her head, with gems and with purple-white shimmerings, and silver jewels in her hair; a cloak of satin around her; a cushion of satin under her; that is how she was.

She had a white rod in her hand, a knife in the other hand, slicing the rod. Every whittle she took from the rod went up and out, as a bright bird, through the window of the tower.

The girl looked at him and said, "Which of us does not wonder at the other, for you wonder at me, and I wonder at you? I am Grian Sun-face, and take you this rod to whittle it a while."

Lusca took hold of the rod and whittled it for a while. With every whittle, every evil and every feebleness that he had met before did not put upon him its hurt, except for the wound of the Big Mokkalve in his side.

"It is a rod never to be whittled away," said Grian Sun-face, "but to be whittled for ever. My father gave it to save me from thinking long."

Lusca was filled with a need to be from the place, for the whittle of the rod was great. He said, "My life is not to be for ever making bright birds." He left the girl in the tower and went back to the shores of the lake, not a hair of his clothing wet on him.

It was only a small time from that out when Lusca passed from the island into a country where there was neither day nor night but a dusk without moon or stars. No one did he see there, there were no creatures, but the land lay in a sweat of hideousness and the trees were broken. High on a hill there was a castle, and in it Lusca found no people except a white-haired warrior, a beardless lad, and an ancient bent grey coughing woman. Between them they had a ball of black iron in the fire round which they lay.

Lusca sat down at the fire, and when he sat down the iron ball turned through blackness to redness in the fire, and the people there rose up and gave Lusca three kisses. Lusca said, "What is that din of dinging I hear?"

"Take you a blessing and a victory for freeing us," said the white-haired warrior, "and it is Shasval the Smith."

"I do not free you," said Lusca. He rose and went from the castle to where the din of dinging was. He found a cave, and before it a dark smith at a red forge, hammering a Sword of Light.

Lusca said, "The Big Mokkalve opened the gate of my side and I must get healing."

The smith answered nothing and hammered the sword.

Lusca went back to the castle and sat near the fire. The ball of iron there turned through blackness to redness and the warrior, the lad and the woman gave him three kisses. "Take a blessing and a victory for your coming, and free us from fear," said the warrior.

"I do not free you," said Lusca. He went out again to the smith. "The Big Mokkalve opened the gate of my side and I must get healing."

The smith answered nothing and hammered the sword.

Lusca went to the castle and sat near the fire. The ball of iron turned through blackness to redness and the warrior, the lad and the woman gave him three kisses.

"Take a blessing and a victory for your coming," said the warrior. "Isbernya is the land in which you are now. There visited us a worm, and she swallowed our heavy flocks and our people after them, and she slaughtered our hosts, both young and old, so that none are alive except the three you see here. But our wise men left prophecy for us, that when the ball in the fire should turn through blackness to redness, Lusca, son of the King of Irrua, should come to free us from fear and to slay that wonderful worm."

Lusca was attended, nobly and honourably. The old warrior said, "Son of Irrua, I and that lad have the same father, and the woman there is our mother, and we are of one birth. But poison was the first food given to the lad; whoever is reared upon poison at the first, neither age nor harm affect him through time eternal."

Lusca said, "Let me be shown the way to that mighty worm."

Lusca and the lad went to where the worm was. They found her looking about to go round the castle, trying if she could get in. When she was not able to get in, she coiled herself on the castle. Lusca gave a cast of a royal javelin that was in his hand at the worm, so that he sent the spear through her and through two windows of the castle and through the coil on the other side. There was the worm, unable to loose herself. Then Lusca took his sword and cut the head from her. The blood made the blade green.

Great joy of that worm seized the warrior, the lad and the woman. They flung their arms about Lusca; but he felt his life going from him with the wound of the Big Mokkalve.

Lusca went and said to the smith, "I must get healing."

The smith said, "Who are you to come here? A boatful of blood has gone from your side. Bigger things have been stopped."

The smith took ointment to the wound of the Big Mokkalve. The side healed.

"The gate of my side is bolted," said Lusca. "The blue mouth is closed. If there is the Great Dug of the World, it must be with you."

"The Great Dug of the World," said the smith, "is not with me. The Great Dug of the World is at the Forest of Wonders. Do not go after it. The way of the forest is this: there is a Tree of Splendour in the forest, and one of every colour on that tree. There is no fruit of the fruits of life that is not on that tree, and it is hard for any man who sees it to part from it for its marvellous splendour. No man has ever gone into that forest who ever came out of it again for its enchantment. Do not look for the Dug, till the womb of judgment or the end of life."

"Even if you were to have the Great Dug with you now," said Lusca, "I would not go from here without seeing this forest, for your report of it. But who is the master of the Sword of Light?"

The smith said, "It is for Lurga Lom to take with him on the day that he shall go against the City of the Red Stream. Until that day, he shall not know it: but, on that day, it shall know him."

"Where is the Forest of Wonders?" said Lusca.

"The Forest of Wonders is far from you," said the smith. "Beware of the Forest of Wonders. There is no hideous thing in hollow nor in the dreadful clouds of air that will not come to you then. It is impossible to count or to tell all the evil and the confusion of enchantment that will be in the forest at the joint of that hour."

"No more the less shall I go there," said Lusca, and departed.

It was then Lusca faced for the Forest of Wonders. He saw at a distance from him the Tree of Virtues. He saw the colours and the fruits beneath the branches wide-sweeping of that flower-marvellous tree.

He found thirteen men on the outskirts of the forest, lacking heads, and in the middle of them lay a king-warrior, a mantle of fair gold about him, clustering golden hair and a diadem of gold on the head by the body. Lusca never beheld the same number of men who were more remarkable than that dead band.

There was a sandal of gold on the foot of the hero, and Lusca stretched out his hand to take it, but the foot cast him over seven ridges from it backwards. Then the head of the body spoke.

"This time yesterday," said the head, "no man could have insulted that foot."

"Head?" said Lusca. "Have you speech?"

"I have," said the head.

"What is the story?" said Lusca.

"Dig a grave for my men and me," said the head, "and you shall get the story."

Lusca dug with the great broad spear that he had near his shield.

"The grave is ready," said the head.

"It is ready now," said Lusca.

"Gold-arm Iollan is the man whose head I am," said the head, "son of the King of the Birds. I could not but go to seek the Tree of Virtues, and my twelve foster-brothers came with me. But enchantment was worked upon us here: for the first we saw was a musical harper walking in the forest, and the little man reached over his fist and struck the man of us who was nearest him between the nose and the mouth, and that man drew his sword to strike the musical harper, but it was not the harper he struck but the man next to himself; so that it was ourselves we beheaded, one after one, through the spells of the musical harper, and he took off the head of the last man with my own sword. But what marvel is that? There is many a greater marvel in the Forest of Wonders."

Lusca put his hands around Gold-arm Iollan and laid him in the grave. He placed six on each side of him and covered them with earth.

After that work, Lusca looked at the forest until he saw a musical harper coming towards him, his harp with him, a rusty sword by his side. Lusca gave a leap at the harper without speaking, and smashed the harp on the rock of stone that was nearest him, sending fragments of the harp into every fifth of the forest. The musical harper gathered up the harp again, piece after piece, so that it seemed that neither stroke nor blow had ever touched it. Lusca took the harper and lifted his head from his body, but the little man departed with his head in his hand by the hair, his harp in the other hand, into the forest; and Lusca marvelled at that.

It was not long after the little man had gone that Lusca saw a wild ox. He smote a blow on it.

And there was never cat nor hag
Nor hideous senseless spectre
In crag nor in hollow

Nor in rock nor in house
Nor on land nor in the dreadful clouds of air
But came at the roar of that ox.

Lusca passed a hand round his great broad spear
that was beside his shield. He gave a cast of it, so that
he sent it through the ox. When the spear reached it,
not greater was the screaming of any other beast than
the screaming of the spear itself; and Lusca marvelled
at the nature of that spear.

This is how the creatures of the forest were in that
hour:

Some scream and
Some bellow and
Some moan and
Some of them stamp the ground
With their heads and their feet.

It is impossible to count or to tell all the evil and
the confusion of enchantment that was in the forest
at the joint of that hour, for there was neither stone
nor tree in it but was in one shaking and in one
thunder.

Lusca took out a venomous stone that was in the
hollow of his shield, and he collected the senseless
creatures, until he drove them into the mouth of a
cave in the forest; and it had been a good cause of
confusion to a bad hero in the Forest of Wonders at
that time to be listening to the wailing, the
screeching, the tremulous bellowing of those
many-shaped spectres.

Lusca came back through the forest after that

work, tired, anxious, sorrowful; and many was the wandering wolf nimbly-going, rising up on every side of him. He did not overtake them, but they were going away from him in every fifth of the forest, in quick running throngs.

Lusca called with a loud great clear voice, "Not better would I like a sleeping-couch, if I had it tonight, than to be fighting with the monsters of this forest!" Then he went to the Tree of Virtues, and he bore off with him a great shoulder-load of the branches of that blossom-haunted tree, so that he made of it a hut in the forest. It was not under the protection of the forest that Lusca went that night, but of his own hand and of his own blade.

He blew a fire heap.

> And it was the rushing of red wind
> Or sound of wave down jagged waterfall
> The wailing of the creatures
> The sound of a great wind against rough hills
> Eyes in their heads like stars.

But that rock, Lusca, son of the King of Irrua, was unchanged in shape or sense or form, his speech unwandering, listening to great evils.

He went a second time and gave a hand about the creatures, so that he drove them into the same cave again. He followed them up the bed of the cave, and there is no knowledge of what direction they went from him then.

Lusca came back. It seemed to him that none the less for all the loss of creatures he wrought was the malignity of the forest. He came to the fire. He did not find one spark of it alive, nor a hut, but a close coppice oak-wood of thin trees, smooth and very high, and bitter quick venomous winds, and wet, heavy snow bending those trees and cold linns of spring water welling there.

It could not be told then all the destruction of enchantment that was throughout the Forest of Wonders.

Next Lusca met a giant, with two grey goat horns through his skull. A round, black hand he had, and one leg like the mast of a ship under him.

"What news?" said Lusca.

"I have no mind to tell news," said the giant, "except only this. It was night-straying that brought me into the forest."

Lusca gave a stroke of his sword through the giant's head, and the sound of the giant was the noise of an oak falling. But the giant gave a twist to his body until he came standing again on the one leg, the sword through his head, Lusca on his shoulder with two hands in the grip of the sword that could not let go.

Then Lusca took hold firmly and squeezed. He made little fragments of the handle and fell off backwards from the shoulder of the giant to the ground. He turned his head. This is what he saw: a pillar of stone, the sword through it from one side to the other.

He climbed the stone, but he could not draw out

the sword, so he went back through the forest to the coppice of thin trees. He found both trees and earth in one slab of ice. It was not a good camp for him to stay that night.

"I am a stranger," said Lusca, "and I have come a long way to be at the Forest of Wonders, but I shall not be the better for it, if I am alive tomorrow."

He did not know what to do. The water of the forest was as cold as drowned sally; the air was full of ghosts, so that if a kindred friend had come close to a man he would not hear him for the talk and the shouting.

"It is not a danger to me," said Lusca. "They are not things of fight or conflict."

He saw a shining lamp lit up, a girl bearing the lamp, and that the girl was Grian Sun-face, from the gold tower under the lake.

She said, "Come with me to my father's castle. He is the King of the Forest of Wonders. The Great Dug of the World is with him."

The King of the Forest of Wonders rose up and took Lusca by the hand and put him sitting in the king's place.

"Who is the young hero?" said the king to Grian Sun-face.

"Lusca, son of the King of Irrua, is that man," she said, "and give him everything he shall ask of you, for he is able to take it against your will. Though your hosts are many they are very little in his hands, for it was by him that the battle was broken on the

Big Mokkalve in the Lands of Sorcha. Many, too, were the horrors of your forest, yet they fell by him. It is better to give him everything he shall ask of you."

"What thing will he ask?" said the king.

"I am sure that he is on the track of the Great Dug of the World," said Grian Sun-face.

"It is well we did not meet at the beginning of this night," said the king. "But now what good thing would you have of the forest?"

"The thing I would have is the Great Dug of the World," said Lusca.

"The Great Dug of the World is not with me," said the king. "The Cat of the Free Isle has it, for she brought it away before you, to make alive again the Kurrirya Crookfoot and your two brothers."

"Sweet is that to hear," said Lusca, and he went straight to the battle-hill in the Lands of Sorcha, Grian Sun-face with him.

They found the hag, sitting by the fire, the Great Dug of the World next to her, and the dead Kurrirya next to that, in the grave of green cresses. But of the cat or of his brothers Lusca had no sign.

The hag said, "This hill is my hill, and the man who makes fire on my hill is my man; and I must have ransom of gold or ransom of the head of the man himself or would you spend this night with me?"

"Lay aside your silly talk," said Lusca. "Where are my brothers?"

"The Cat of the Free Isle made them alive," said the hag. "They have gone after her to find the place where she is in."

Lusca knelt by the Kurrirya.

The hag said, "Get him from uselessness: up from dreaming."

He took the Great Dug of the World and bathed the Kurrirya with the stuff that was in it.

The hag said, "Where life ran let words come. Join the silver bone: bond the gold vein. Drench death down."

The Kurrirya rose up as whole and as healthy as he had ever been.

Lusca said, "My foster-brother and my kindred friend. And the gate of my side is closed."

"The woman you must find," said the Kurrirya, "is at the City of the Red Stream. I came through the world and death to give you this; but you did not, and you would not, as I told you."

"And me you left," said the hag.

Lusca made a look at the hag. She changed misshape for shapeliness before him. She stood, Behinya, the treasure of a woman, sister to Bright-eyed Faylinn, the Cat of the Free Isle.

Then they welcomed each other in words of the olden time, kissed lovingly and told their adventures from first to last.

"Now tell me of the city," said Lusca.

The Kurrirya said, "Here is how the city is: there are three chieftain streams around it, and they are in a crimson-lit flame. For the heat and the fire no man dare approach the city. Whoever sees it will never have his health from all the flame and the heat. Every evil that ever was met was good when put against the ills of that city. In the city is the woman. That is the place where she is in."

Lusca, the Kurrirya, Behinya and Grian Sun-face then took the good and the ill of it upon themselves and put the ship out over the back-ridges of each deep sea till they came to the City of the Red Stream.

They found the big brother and the little brother of Lusca sitting outside the walls of the city by the three chieftain streams of flame. The brothers had taken all the third plunder division of the world on their way to the city, but the city itself they could not reach for the full-red lake.

"There are no men in it," said the big brother, "except a hundred only; and they are the Kings of the World."

"But there are three thousand women in it," said the little brother. "Over them all is the woman we must find."

"It is by the women," said the big brother, "that the greater portion of valour of life is remembered. Great is the fear, even for you, from them."

They bore away that night until the morning of the morrow, until the day shone with its fierce light. Yet no less for that were the flames about the city burning.

There came out over the walls of the city Bright-eyed Faylinn. She had a cloak about her, the clustering hair over her shoulder, two spears of fire in her hand.

Then Lusca struck a shield blow and a fight kindling upon his shield. Faylinn said, "I never left corner nor country, nor islet nor island, on sea or on land, but I visited there; yet I never heard the like of that shield blow, for the whole city is in one quivering and one thunder."

The Kurrirya said, "Lusca is here, and his two brothers are here, the sons of the King of Irrua; and Grian Sun-face, daughter of the King of the Forest of Wonders, and Behinya, your own half-sister, and I, the Kurrirya; I am here."

Faylinn said, "No greater for that is the heed that we pay them."

"Do not speak foolish and unprofitable words," said the Kurrirya. "Except for the red stream you would know the strong man; the blue candle of valour, the right hand of heroes, the battle-prop of countries and the sustaining warrant of all; the king-tree of heroism, the mind without turning; Lusca, son of Dolvath, son of Libren, son of Loman, son of Cas, son of Tag of the kindred of Irrua."

Faylinn said, "No greater for that is the heed that we pay them. You have not the crossing of the red stream."

Lusca said, "What brings the wonderful heat into this flood beyond every other flood?"

Faylinn said, "I think it friendly to let you know it. Seven stones I have in that stream. It is a part of their virtue that whatever stream or river-mouth in which they are placed shall always turn to be a blaze of flame, so long as the stones shall be in it."

Lusca said, "Is there anything that would prevent the heat of this full-red lake?"

Faylinn said, "I think it friendly to let you know it. There is knowledge and prophecy for us that a man shall come and shall quench the fire in our despite. Against him the flames shall grow cold. But the man is not Lusca, nor his big brother, nor his little brother, nor the Kurrirya Crookfoot. The man is Lurga Lom."

Lusca heard this, and a fist upon manhood, a fist upon strengthening, a fist upon power went into him. He said, "If ever the earth has put on the ridge of its back such a man, let me see him." He went from the city in the power of the sharp-travelling wind to the Upland of Grief in Isbernya, to the forge and the cave of Shasval the Smith. He stood at the cave and said, "Where is Lurga Lom?"

The smith said nothing and hammered a Sword of Light.

Lusca said, "Where is Lurga Lom?"

The smith said nothing and hammered the sword.

Lusca said, "Where is Lurga Lom?"

The smith said, "The sword is ready. Have you come?"

Lusca cast about him to find a man, but there was no man in that place if not himself.

The smith said, "The sword is ready. Have you come?"

Lusca cast about him again to find a man, but there was no man if not himself.

The smith said, "Have you come?"

Lusca took a step to the sword. He said, "And if I am not Lurga Lom." He reached the sword. He said, "Yet I have come." And the sword knew him.

Lusca went from there in the power of the sharp-travelling wind till he came again to the City of the Red Stream, the Sword of Light in his hand. He trod the brown flames and the stream was at once made cold and dried up, so that Lusca and his people crossed by the seven stones over to the city and gave shortness of life to all they found in it, except to the Kings of the World and to Faylinn alone.

It was then that Lusca was freed from his crosses and his spells; and Lurga Lom he became from that time out. His big brother took Behinya, and his little brother took Grian Sun-face, and he himself took to him Bright-eyed Faylinn, the Cat of the Free Isle; and they agreed.

The Kurrirya Crookfoot wrote this story in poet's wands: it is the fifth language into which it has been made.

And the Kings of the World were sent to their lands.